A Mole Home

by Liza Charlesworth

ISBN: 978-1-338-84442-9

Art Director: Tannaz Fassihi; Designer: Cynthia Ng; Illustrated by Michael Robertson
Copyright © Liza Charlesworth. All rights reserved. Published by Scholastic Inc.

3 4 5 6   68   26 25 24

Printed in Jiaxing, China. First printing, June 2022.

It is Cole.
Cole is a sad mole.
Cole is alone in his home!

2

So Cole said,
"I hope I can get
a nice new home."

3

"I see a rose!" said Cole.
Is a rose a mole home?
NOPE!

4

"I see a cone!" said Cole.
Is a cone a mole home?
NOPE!

"I see a hose!" said Cole.
Is a hose a mole home?

NOPE, NOPE, NOPE!

"I see a note!" said Cole.
It said, *Run on the stones
to get a nice new home.*

So Cole ran on the stones.
Run, run, run.
They led to a big hole.

Poke!
Cole put his nose
in the big hole.

"I see A LOT of moles!"
said Cole.
A hole IS a mole home!

Time to read jokes
to moles in a big hole.
HEE, HEE, HEE!

Cole is not sad.
Cole is not alone.
Cole has a nice new home!

13

Read & Review

Invite your learner to point to each long-*o* word and read it aloud.

hope

mole

jokes

Cole

note

14

nope

hose

cone

rose   moles

alone

stones   hole

home

poke

nose

Fun Fill-Ins

Read the sentences aloud, inviting your learner to complete them using the long-*o* words in the box.

hose   mole   hole   home   Cole

1. This story is about a mole named _____.
2. Cole wanted to get a new _____.
3. Cole did not want his home to be a rose, cone, or _____.
4. Cole ran on some stones, which led to a big _____.
5. A hole is a nice home for a _____!